WHAT HAPPENED?

SWITCHBACK SWITCHEROO

Book design by Jake Slavik
Illustrations by Courtney Huddleston

Design Elements: Shutterstock Images

Published in the United States by Jolly Fish Press, an imprint of North Star Editions, Inc.

First Edition
First Printing, 2020

This is a work of fiction. Names, characters, places, and incidents are either the product of the author's imagination or are used fictitiously, and any resemblance to actual persons living or dead, business establishments, events, or locales is entirely coincidental.

Library of Congress Cataloging-in-Publication Data (pending)
978-1-63163-420-8 (paperback)
978-1-63163-419-2 (hardcover)

Jolly Fish Press
North Star Editions, Inc.
2297 Waters Drive
Mendota Heights, MN 55120
www.jollyfishpress.com

Printed in the United States of America

WHAT HAPPENED?

SWITCHBACK
SWITCHEROO

by VERITY WEAVER

illustrated by COURTNEY HUDDLESTON

text by JENNIFER MOORE

Chapter 1

THE SWITCHEROO

Saturday, April 30, 11:55 a.m.

Nothing exciting ever happened in the sleepy town of Switchington Falls . . . until Switchback Day! There was a lively carnival feel about the place today, with loud music blaring out of speakers all around Polestone Park and a dancing procession of Switchback fans streaming toward the newly built performance hall and outdoor stage. Everyone had turned out to watch the grand opening, from babies in strollers to old ladies with walkers, all jigging along to the catchy beat of Switchback's number one hit, "Losing My Head Over You."

The kids of Switchington Falls Middle School were out in full force too, hoping to catch a glimpse of their school's famous ex-pupil. It was funny to think of Switchback (or Taz Clifton, as he was known back then) doing math and English lessons in the same classrooms they sat in every day. Funny to think of him eating the same soggy lunches in the school cafeteria and listening to the same boring lectures from old Mr. Longdrone, who'd been the principal there for as long as anyone could remember. Mr. Longdrone wasn't his usual boring self today, though, despite his dull gray suit and matching clip-on tie. Not even his boring work outfit could protect him from the Switchback fever sweeping through the town. There he was, bouncing and bopping to the pounding beat like an overexcited teenager.

"Cool moves, Mr. L!" called Mishka and Catalina, squeezing and wriggling their way toward the front of the crowd for a better view of the big screen, with Mishka's dad trailing somewhere behind. It wasn't just a big screen. It was an enormous one, towering over the new outdoor stage, promising a perfect view of the grand unveiling ceremony.

"Yeah, nice one, sir," shouted Kai, joining them from the other direction with his little sister balanced on his shoulders, the heels of her sandals rubbing against his faded Zombie Zac T-shirt. "Where'd you learn to dance like that?" He jumped as someone brushed past him and spun around with a worried look on his face.

"You're better than my mom, that's for sure," piped up Jermaine from his prime spot near the stage. His mom was right there beside him, flinging herself around like a demented chicken in a sparkly, sequined SWITCHBACK crop top. Jermaine was trying his best to ignore her, but it wasn't easy.

Mr. Longdrone beamed, his gray moustache quivering in time to the music. "The doctor told me I needed to do more exercise," he told them, shouting to make himself heard above the booming bass. "So my grandson's been giving me street dancing lessons. He helped me pick out some new shoes as well," he added, pointing to the bright-yellow sneakers on his feet. "I see why you kids like them now. *So* much comfier than my stiff work sh—" But the end of his sentence was lost beneath the noisy whir of blades above their heads.

"It's him!" The crowd erupted in a fresh roar of excitement, a sea of expectant faces tilting up toward the sky as a silver helicopter loomed into view. "It's Switchback!"

Yes, Switchback was here. It had been fifteen years since Taz Clifton and his family moved to California, but Switchington Falls's most famous resident was finally back. His private helicopter hovered above the cheering crowd for a minute before circling back around to the landing pad on top of the new performance hall, where the town mayor and local VIPs were waiting. Luckily for the townsfolk, there were camera operators stationed up there too, relaying live-action images of Switchback's arrival to the big screen.

Kai clutched at his sister's ankles, his legs trembling inside his ripped jeans, as the musical megastar cleared the still-whirring helicopter blades. Mishka clutched at Catalina as the camera zoomed in close for a first glimpse of that famous Switchback grin. Catalina clutched at Jermaine as the crowd broke into a welcome-home burst of "Losing My Head Over You," while Jermaine clutched Mr. Longdrone's gray-suited elbow, singing away with everyone else like a proper Switchback fan. And Mr. Longdrone? Mr. Longdrone clutched at his boring old clip-on tie, ripping it off his neck with a wild whoop.

"Go Taz!" he shouted, whirling the tie above his head like a lasso. "I mean, *Yo* Taz!" He dabbed at his eyes with his other hand. "Last time I saw that boy, he was in detention, and now look at him."

The crowd fell silent as Marlene Richards, the town mayor, stepped forward to shake the music star's hand.

"Welcome home, Switchback," she said, her brown eyes sparkling behind her glasses. "On behalf of everyone here, I'd like to say how delighted we are that you'll be opening our new performance hall today."

Mishka let out a whoop of excitement, pointing to the hand-painted I ❤ SWITCHBACK logo on her T-shirt, as if her musical hero would be able to see all the way from up there on the roof. She wasn't whooping as loudly as Mr. Longdrone, though. *No one* was whooping as loudly as him!

Catalina rolled up her sleeves, already regretting her choice of clothes. It was getting hot and sticky in the crowd, with the sun beating down, but she couldn't take off her sweater without revealing the Lisa La Loop top she was wearing underneath. She picked up a dropped newspaper by her feet, with a front-page story about the recent robbery in neighboring Riddlingford Heights, and fanned herself with that instead.

"Thank you, Mayor Richards," said Switchback. "I'm very excited to be here." He looked around at the assembled VIPs and the crowds below. "Yes, it sure is good to be back!"

"And can *I* just say what an honor it is to be here today too," called a shrill voice. A small lady with bright-blue hair elbowed her way through the welcoming committee to reach the cameras.

"Look, it's Picassa!" said Mishka, looking more excited than ever. "That's who I met yesterday."

"For anyone who's not familiar with my work," the lady continued, "I'm Picassa Daygar, award-winning local sculptor and ceramic artist. It's *my* life-size model of Switchback that he'll be unveiling today to mark the opening of the new building. *My* piece of artistic excellence that will be gracing the entrance hall for the people of Switchington Falls to enjoy and appreciate in the years to come. *My* legacy that will live on in the hearts and minds of—"

"Yes, yes, thank you for that detailed introduction," said

Mayor Richards, turning back to Switchback. "As I was saying, we're delighted to have such a famous face with us here today, and I know your many, many fans are looking forward to your live performance after the opening ceremony. So perhaps we should move straight on to the unveiling now," she suggested, guiding him over to the rooftop stairs.

Down in the crowd, a woman in a wide-brimmed hat squeezed her way between Mr. Longdrone and Jermaine. "Thank goodness I made it in time," she gasped. "I can't wait to see this." She wore expensive-looking sunglasses and a flowered scarf pulled up high over her chin. She shuffled along sideways to avoid Catalina's penetrating stare.

"Neither can I," agreed Mishka. "I love art and sculptures, *and* I love Switchback. This is the best day ever."

The camera feed died as the roof party made its way down to the ground floor, sparking back into life a few minutes later in the smart new entrance lobby. It revealed Switchback standing beside a life-size statue covered with a purple velvet curtain. Picassa was there too, telling anyone who would listen about the incredible artistic skills required to produce such an outstanding work of art.

"I'd like to thank you all for inviting me," said Switchback. "If anyone had told twelve-year-old me that I'd be opening this wonderful new building today, I wouldn't have believed them. But here I am, back in the very town that inspired my name.

Switchback's back! And it gives me great pleasure to declare the new Switchington Falls Performance Hall open!"

He tugged aside the velvet covering with a deft flick of his famous fingers to reveal the finest piece of artistic excellence in the entire history of the town . . .

Switchback's cheesy camera grin faded. "Oh! That wasn't quite what I was expecting. My assistant said it was going to be a statue of *me*." He turned around, scanning the crowded lobby. "Where *is* she anyway? Has anyone seen Suki?"

"Forget about Suki," came a shrill cry from behind. The camera shifted to Picassa Daygar's tight lips and wild, staring eyes. "Where's my statue? My masterpiece? My legacy? All those weeks of work," she squeaked, her voice rising higher than ever. "What's happened to my wonderful statue?"

"You mean, that's not it?" asked Switchback. He looked relieved to hear it. "I thought it might be some weird arty thing—some clever comment about how the rest of the world sees me."

Picassa grabbed hold of the unveiled object and shook it. "Does this *look* like a clever comment to you? Like the greatest piece of art this town has ever seen? Of course it doesn't. It's a coat rack, you numbskull. A CHEAP, UGLY COAT RACK!"

Whoa, thought Jermaine, as the cameras zoomed in closer. *What was* that *doing there?* He stole a sly, sideways glance at his mother. She wasn't dancing around like a sequined chicken anymore—she was staring at the screen along with everyone else, murmuring something about her book club.

Book club? Oh no. It couldn't be. Could it?

Jermaine clutched at Mr. Longdrone's elbow again, steadying himself against the sudden rush of panic coursing through his veins.

Please tell me I'm wrong, he thought, turning back to the screen, hoping for a simple explanation to the statue–coat rack switcheroo. One that didn't include book clubs.

On the screen, Mayor Richards stepped forward. "There would appear to be a bit of a mix-up. If you'd like to put the coat rack back down, Picassa . . ."

But the artist was too busy screaming to listen. "Look at it!" she shrieked. "It's hideous! I've never been so insulted in my life! Where's my statue? WHO'S STOLEN MY PRECIOUS STATUE?"

Mishka gave a little start. "Stolen, did she say?" *Does that mean I was right all along?*

"I think so," said Catalina, only she wasn't looking at the screen. She was too busy staring at the woman in the wide-brimmed hat and pulled-up scarf.

"Of course!" murmured Kai to himself. "It all makes sense now." And then he muttered something about broken teeth and police officers, which didn't make any sense at all.

Back on the big screen, a pair of burly bodyguards in dark glasses and black puffer jackets were wrestling the coat rack away from the hysterical sculptor. Mayor Richards smiled for the cameras, doing her best to reassure the crowds outside that everything was under control.

But no one was fooled. The missing statue wasn't just a hiccup in the opening ceremony—it was a downright disaster.

"What if they can't find it?" asked Kai's little sister, sounding upset. "Will Switchback still do his concert for us?"

"The concert's the least of his worries," replied Kai, looking around with a panicked expression. He shivered in the noon sun. "The least of *anyone's* worries. That statue was only the warm-up. A practice. We need to warn Switchback and get out of here while we still can."

"Leave now, you mean?" asked Mishka, listening in. "Before we hear him sing?" She shook her head in disbelief. "No way!"

Chapter 2

Mishka, Friday, April 29, 2:00 p.m.

Twenty-two hours to go! What was that in minutes? I pulled my calculator out of my bag to check. One thousand three hundred and twenty. Which was only seventy-nine thousand two hundred seconds. *Oh my goodness, oh my goodness. Less than eighty thousand seconds until I see Switchback!*

No wonder I was having trouble concentrating in class. Not even art—my favorite class of all—could keep my mind off his arrival. We were supposed to be painting a portrait of someone famous (no prizes for guessing who I'd chosen!), but my version of Switchback was a poor imitation of the real thing. I couldn't seem to get his hair right (the more I tried, the worse it got), and the silver suit I'd painted made him look more like a fish than a pop star.

Ooh, I thought, absentmindedly chewing the end of my paintbrush. *I hope he's wearing his silver suit tomorrow. The light-up one from the "Losing My Head Over You" video. I'll have to get a good spot near the front so I can snap some photos. And I can't forget my T-shirt—I wonder if Switchback will be able to see it from the stage?*

"Mishka?"

I was dimly aware of someone calling me, but my brain was in full daydream mode. I imagined it was Switchback, picking me out from the crowd. *Mishka!* he said, magically knowing my name even though we'd never met. *That's a fantastic T-shirt you've got there—you're so clever to have painted it yourself. Why don't you join me up here for the next song so everyone can see it?*

"Mishka?"

There it was again. This time it was the crowds, cheering me on as I made my way up onto the stage. Catalina was there with me, even though she's not a proper Switchback fan, and we were doing our special Double Duck routine—the one we invented at the last school dance—and then Switchback joined in too, making

it a *Triple* Duck dance! The crowds *really* loved that. They were cheering so loud that Switchback invited us to join his backup dancers at his next concert . . . and then . . . and then . . .

"Hello? Earth to Mishka?"

"Huh?" The cheering crowds melted away, and my musical hero turned back into a half-finished painting on my desk. That's when I spotted Miss Monnay standing over me with a concerned look on her face.

"Are you all right?" she asked. "You've been staring into space for the last ten minutes."

Had I? That meant it was only one thousand three hundred and ten minutes left until Switchback arrived!

"And that paintbrush you're sucking . . ."

Paintbrush? What paintbrush? Oh, that *one.* It wasn't until I pulled it out of my mouth that I realized I'd been sucking the wrong end. *Yuck!*

"Perhaps you could use the water provided to clean it next time," said Miss Monnay, smiling as I wiped the paint off my mouth with a tissue. "Dear me, you're not really with us today, are you?"

One thousand three hundred and nine . . .

"Too busy thinking about tomorrow, I'm guessing?"

"Yes," I admitted, feeling bad. I thought of Mr. Longdrone's long, droning lecture in assembly that morning, about keeping our minds on our work even though we were excited. It was a good thing he couldn't see me now. Then I thought of the *Mona Lisa* picture on my T-shirt and felt even worse. Leonardo da Vinci had never let pop star daydreams come between him and his art, had he? Or Michelangelo. I bet they'd never painted people with terrible hair and fish outfits either, or sucked the wrong end of the paintbrush. "Sorry, Miss Monnay."

"Taz was a terrible daydreamer too," said Miss Monnay. "Too busy planning out his glittering music career to concentrate on art."

"Taz Clifton, you mean? Switchback? You actually knew him?"

Miss Monnay nodded. "Oh yes, I remember him well. He used to sit right there, in fact, where you're sitting now."

"Here?" *Oh my goodness. Oh my goodness. I'm never sitting anywhere else again!*

"I used to hear him humming under his breath, even after I'd told the class to be quiet. Oh yes, that boy was always humming. It's funny to think some of those tunes might have grown into world-famous hits."

"And are you still in touch with him now?" I asked. Maybe Miss Monnay could introduce us after the concert. How amazing would that be? Maybe I really *would* get to show him the I ♥ SWITCHBACK T-shirt I'd spent all last weekend making. "Will you be seeing him tomorrow?"

"Oh no, I don't think he'd remember me after all this time. Art wasn't exactly his favorite subject. And I'm away tomorrow, which is a shame. I'd have liked to see the unveiling of the new statue. But I promised my friend in the city I'd visit, and she's got a whole weekend of art galleries planned out." Miss Monnay sighed. "That's if they're still open with this gang of art thieves on the loose."

"Art thieves?" For a moment I forgot about Switchback. Forgot about T-shirts and cheering crowds and Double Duck dancing to the most amazing songs on the planet. "What do you mean?"

"The Meaner Lisa gang," said Miss Monnay. "That's what the press are calling them—like the *Mona Lisa*," she said, pointing to my T-shirt, "only meaner. They've been targeting museums right across the state, making off with thousands and thousands of dollars' worth of art."

What? How come I hadn't heard about that? Surely they'd have mentioned something like that on the news? Maybe they had. Maybe I'd been too wrapped up in Switchback's visit—too busy counting down the weeks, days, and hours until his arrival—to notice.

"Do you think they'll come here?" I asked. "To the

Switchington Falls Art Gallery?" I was thinking of Mr. Angelo, the white-haired gallery guard who worked there. He was one of the nicest people I knew, with a smile and a chat for everyone, but he was getting old now, and his knees creaked when he got up off his special seat in the corner. I couldn't imagine him chasing after a gang of dangerous criminals and wrestling some priceless picture out of their thieving clutches. I didn't want to imagine it. Poor old Mr. Angelo wouldn't stand a chance.

Miss Monnay looked properly worried for a moment, although perhaps she'd just spotted the paint-flicking fight on the other side of the classroom. "Dear me," she said. "I hope not."

Chapter 3

Mishka, 3:45 p.m.

One thousand two hundred and fifteen minutes left!

"Wait, what are we doing here?" I asked, looking up in surprise as the car pulled into the art gallery parking lot.

Mom grinned at me in the rearview mirror. "I thought maybe you could do with a distraction from the Switchback countdown for an hour or so. I know *I* can. And where better than here?"

Mom and I always went to the gallery when we wanted some quiet time together. It was one of my favorite places in the world, containing as many happy memories as works of art. An after-school trip to the art gallery seemed like a great idea to me. It would make the time go quicker too.

"Good thinking," I told Mom, wondering if the annual local artists' exhibition had started yet. That was always good. And perhaps I should warn Mr. Angelo about the art thieves while we were there too, just in case they decided to pay Switchington Falls a visit. It's not like there were any world-famous paintings at our little gallery—no Van Goghs or Rembrandts or anything like that—but there were a couple of signed Andy Warhol prints and an early sketch by Whistler. They must be worth a bit of money.

We started off in the café (which is where all good visits to the gallery start) with creamy hot chocolates and peanut butter cookies. Then we headed upstairs to see Mr. Angelo.

"Hello there," he said, beaming from ear to ear. "What a lovely surprise. And how are my two favorite ladies today?"

"Good, thanks, Mr. Angelo," I said, sneaking a look over his shoulder for any lurking thieves. Not that I really knew what an art thief looked like. "How are you?"

"Not bad," said Mr. Angelo, still smiling. "Apart from the weak knee and the—" He broke off as Mom's phone started ringing.

"Gosh, I'm sorry," she said. "I meant to switch it on silent when we came in." Mom glanced at the screen and sighed. "Oh dear, it's work again. I'd better get this. Will you be all right on your own for a bit, Mishka, if I take this call outside?"

"Of course," I told her. I wasn't *really* on my own anyway. Not with Mr. Angelo and all of my favorite pictures there to keep me company. "Take as long as you need."

Mom hurried off, murmuring into her phone as she went, leaving me to talk art thefts with Mr. Angelo.

"The Meaner Lisa gang?" he asked. "Oh yes, I've heard of them, all right. A clever bunch, by all accounts, especially when it comes to security systems. They stole an entire oil painting last week—frame and all—from a little gallery upstate. In broad daylight!" Mr. Angelo sounded more impressed than scared. "Almost as daring as the *Mona Lisa* theft back in 1911," he said, pointing to my T-shirt. "The thief disguised himself as one of the Louvre gallery workers and hid until the museum shut for the night, leaving him free to steal the painting. Then all he had to do was smuggle it out under his smock the next morning when the gallery reopened. The *Mona Lisa* wasn't seen again for two years."

"You don't think the gang will strike here though, do you?" I asked.

Mr. Angelo laughed. "Not if it means disguising themselves as the resident gallery guard. They'd have to dye their hair white and work on their creaky knees before anyone mistook them for me!" He glanced up at the clock and heaved himself onto his feet.

"Look at that, four fifteen already. I think it's coffee and fruitcake time. Let's hope those pesky thieves don't show up while I'm on my break," he said with a wink. "Let me know if you spot anyone with a statue under their shirt!"

Four fifteen? That's another thirty minutes gone already!

Mr. Angelo shuffled off in search of refreshments while I headed into the next room to check out the local artists' exhibition. According to the sign on the door, the official opening wasn't until tomorrow, but I could see people in there already. I figured it was okay to have a quick peek. I was a local artist too, after all, even if I didn't have any pictures up on the wall just yet.

"Such smooth lines and beautifully sculpted curves," said an excitable blue-haired woman at the far end of the room. She was waving her arms around wildly as she described the statue beside her. "And exquisite attention to detail as always," she added, her shrill voice booming around the quiet room.

I didn't know who she was talking to, because the elderly-looking couple I'd spotted through the door were already on their way back out, and the only other person in the room was me.

But the lack of an audience didn't seem to put her off at all, her voice growing louder and shriller as she warmed to her subject. "Just look at the texture on those toenails. The hint of fluff in the belly button. The delicate glistening of wax inside the ears . . . *Ex-quis-ite*," she said again, stretching the word out to three times its normal length.

I wasn't sure what to do. Turn around and make my escape while I still could, or check out this statue for myself, hoping Mom would rescue me before the woman got *really* carried away? Before she forced me to admire the *exquisite* boogers up the poor statue's nose? To be honest though, the other exhibits in the room were a bit disappointing (it seemed to be mainly watercolor landscapes and oil paintings of fruit this year), and I wasn't feeling as inspired by my visit as usual. Perhaps the statue would change my mind, I decided, edging toward the other end of the room for a closer look.

It turned out to be a ceramic sculpture of a man in swimming trunks, his hands stretched high in the air as if he was catching an invisible beach ball. I didn't venture near enough to admire the texture of his toenails or the exquisite glistening of his earwax, but the sculpture was clearly the best work of art in the room. Much better than the funny blob picture beside it, which didn't look like anything at all.

"A true masterpiece, I'm sure you'll agree," said the woman. She stopped waving her arms around and started stroking the statue's head instead. "Such lifelike curls. Such bounce, such shine . . ."

My mouth dropped open. What was she doing? Stroking sculptures in an art gallery was strictly forbidden—*everyone* knew

that. Didn't they? Okay, so there might not be any actual signs up warning people to keep their hands off, no list of rules pinned to the wall, but that shouldn't matter. Touching artworks was one of those things you just didn't do, like playing football in church, or cleaning your muddy dog in the swimming pool. Rubbing your grubby hands all over a priceless work of art was like turning up at a glamorous wedding in a caveman outfit, or farting in front of the president. What would Mr. Angelo say when he noticed fingerprints all over the sculpture? And what if she stroked it so hard she knocked the whole thing over?

"Don't you agree?" asked the woman.

"Who, m-me?" I stammered. Should I say something or not? The last thing I wanted was Mr. Angelo getting into trouble if something happened to the statue. But I didn't want to seem rude, either. Mrs. Blue Hair might not take kindly to lectures from a fifth grader. "S-Sorry, what was the question again?"

"I was simply musing on the lifelike springiness to the hair," she said. "Sometimes I'm amazed at my own genius."

"You mean *you're* the artist? That's *your* statue?"

"Of course," said the woman. "There's only one Picassa Daygar."

Wait, I knew that name from somewhere. Had I seen her work at the gallery before?

"I was just checking on the placing of my piece before the

exhibition starts," Picassa explained. "You're lucky to have got in here today, before all my other fans arrive. Once the world sees my Switchback statue tomorrow, they'll be clamoring for more of my work."

Yes! That was it! Picassa Daygar was the local artist they'd commissioned to make the Switchback statue. *That's* why the name sounded so familiar.

"Did you actually get to meet him?" I asked. That would make her the luckiest artist in the world. "Did he model for you while you were sculpting?"

Picassa raised one eyebrow at me in a disapproving fashion. "If you're referring to the singer—the subject of my latest piece—then no, he didn't have the pleasure of working directly with me, I'm afraid. With my level of artistic skill, I can work from photographs alone. But I've no doubt he's looking forward to meeting me tomorrow."

"So you'll actually get to talk to him? To shake his hand?" *Wow! Imagine that!* If only *I'd* been commissioned to provide some art for the grand opening. If only they wanted a painting of Switchback dressed as a fish (with crazy hedgehog hair) to decorate the new building.

Picassa didn't seem to understand how lucky she was. "Yes," she said. "I expect he's counting down the minutes until the grand unveiling even as we speak. Not everyone gets to be immortalized in clay by Picassa Daygar, you know. I just hope they're taking proper care of my statue down there at the performance hall. If anything happens to it, I'll . . . I'll . . ."

I never got to hear *what* she'd do if her precious Switchback sculpture was damaged, because she'd just spotted two more people coming in through the door. Which meant a fresh audience for her one-woman Picassa Daygar appreciation show.

Chapter 4

Mishka, 4:30 p.m.

"A true masterpiece, I'm sure you'll agree," said Picassa, trying to attract the attention of the peculiar-looking men who'd just walked in.

Their matching outfits (Metropolitan Museum of Art T-shirts teamed with paint-splattered pants) looked two sizes too small for them, and their old-fashioned artist berets were pulled so low over their faces it was a wonder they could see where they were going. Especially as they'd forgotten to take their dark sunglasses off! Maybe they were famous artists too? That's what I thought at first. I thought it might be some kind of disguise, to keep autograph hunters away. Or maybe they were pretend artists on their way to a costume party, looking for some extra inspiration to help them get into character. Either way, the men were too busy drawing in their sketchpads to pay *me* any attention. They were doing a pretty good job of ignoring Picassa too, although she wasn't showing any signs of giving up yet.

"Yes, that's right, gentlemen," she said, as if they were in the middle of a conversation. "It's a Picassa Daygar original. One of my finest creations to date, I'm sure you'll agree. Just look at that exquisite detail. Those hands! Those feet! The individual grains of sand clinging to each hairy toe . . ."

The men continued drawing, comparing notes as they worked.

"And that stray dribble of strawberry ice cream in the corner of his mouth," said Picassa, running her finger across the statue's bottom lip. "Look at it! Just look! It's so lifelike you can almost taste it!"

Oh no, I thought. *She's not going to start licking the thing, is she?*

"It's almost as impressive as the statue they'll be unveiling at the new performance hall tomorrow," said Picassa. "I expect you've heard all about it. They're even bringing that singer in to mark the occasion."

"What's that?" asked the first man, looking up from his

sketchbook. He was tall and thin, with a neatly trimmed beard and a white scar on his cheek. "You mentioned a performance hall?"

"Yes," said Picassa. "A brand-new showcase for my work. That's how *I* like to think of it, anyway. A music-themed exhibition space for my finest piece to date."

"And where is this performance hall, exactly?" asked the other man. He was shorter than his friend, with a large nose and dimpled chin.

Even I knew the answer to that one. "In Polestone Park," I told him. "And Switchback's coming to open it in . . ." *What was it now?* "Just under nineteen and a half hours."

"Really?" The man sounded intrigued. "And your statue's already down there now, is it?" he added, turning back to Picassa.

"I'm afraid so, gentlemen. If you want to see the finest ceramic sculpture in the entire state—in the entire country!—you'll have to wait until tomorrow."

The first man buried his face in his sketchbook, his pencil scribbling away furiously. I couldn't see what he was drawing from where I was standing, but he certainly seemed inspired.

"And I assume there's plenty of security in place?" asked his friend.

I nodded. "I think Switchback has his own team of body-guards." That must be a good job to have as well. Traveling all around the country listening to live performances every night. Not as good as being a famous artist, obviously—that was still my number one plan—but not a bad second choice.

"What about security for the statue though?" he asked. "Do you know anything about that?"

A *statue* bodyguard? I'd never even heard of one of those.

"You don't think anyone would try to *take* it, do you?" gasped Picassa. "Perhaps I should get down there now and make sure everything's okay."

"Oh no," said the first man. "I'm sure that won't be necessary. We were just interested, that's all." He bent over his notebook and started sketching again . . . except now that I thought about it—now that I followed the little up and down movements of his pencil more closely—it looked more like he was writing than drawing. Was he jotting down reviews of the paintings? Were he and his friend secret judges for the Switchington Falls Artist of the Year Award?

Curiosity finally got the better of me. I sidled over, pretending to study a neighboring oil painting of a pineapple as I stole a sideways peek over their shoulders. I couldn't make out many of the words in the first man's sketchbook, apart from "estimated value" and "CCTV cameras." But that was enough to know it wasn't a review of *Pineapple on Plate* by Ana Nas. As for his friend's notebook—well, he really *had* been drawing. Drawing a room

plan of the art gallery. Why on earth would anyone want one of those? Unless . . . Unless they were art thieves planning their next robbery! Of course! That explained the strange disguises too. I had to warn Mr. Angelo before it was too late.

I crept back to the door, sneaking out into the main gallery while Picassa was singing the praises of the hairy mole on her statue's back. But there was no sign of Mr. Angelo—he must still have been on his coffee break. Mom was there though, looking relieved to see me.

"Where have you been?" she asked. "I've been looking all over for you."

"*Shh*." I put a finger to my lips and pointed back to the special exhibition room. "I was in there," I said. "With a crazy sculptor lady and a pair of art thieves. We need to find Mr. Angelo and let him know what's happening. In fact, maybe we should call the police too."

"Oh, Mishka," said Mom, grinning as if it was all a joke. "You do come out with some funny things. I suppose you've been chatting to the queen of England in there too, have you?"

"I'm serious, Mom. It's the Meaner Lisa gang. I know it is. They've been casing out the art gallery, getting ready for their next robbery. *And* they wanted to know about the new Switchback statue down at the performance hall. What if they try to steal that too?"

Perhaps we should ask the police to pass on a warning to Switchback as well. That was my next thought. *And then he'll be so grateful he'll invite me up onstage to dance with him tomorrow.*

Mom wasn't buying it though. "And how do you know they were art thieves? Were they wearing black masks over their eyes, carrying painting-shaped swag bags?"

I shook my head. "No, just caps and sunglasses. And they were carrying sketchbooks." It didn't sound quite so convincing when I said it out loud somehow. "But I peeked at one of the pages, and it was a map of the museum."

"Art students, I expect," said Mom. "From the adult education course up at the high school."

"And they were making notes about security cameras and how much one of the pieces was worth," I added, trying to convince her.

Mom thought for a moment. "Maybe they're professional artists in that case, planning out their next art installation for when that exhibition finishes."

"That's what I thought at first," I admitted. "But there's something funny about them. Something decidedly suspicious."

"We'll mention it to the lady at reception on our way out, if that makes you feel better," said Mom. "Come on, it's time we were getting home anyway. Work called an emergency meeting for tomorrow, and I need to get back and prepare."

Talking to Jamila at reception *did* make me feel better. Much better. She nodded and said, "The two men in berets, you mean? Yes, that's fine, we know all about them. Nothing for you to worry about."

So I stopped worrying, just like she said—they clearly weren't thieves after all—and got back to counting down the hours and minutes until my musical hero arrived instead. *Goodbye, thinking about the Meaner Lisa gang. Hello, dreaming about Switchback!*

Chapter 5

Jermaine, Friday, April 29, 7:25 p.m.

Mishka once told me "Losing My Head Over You" was all about Switchback's secret girlfriend. But lately, all I could think about when I heard that song was Mom. She'd been losing her head over Switchback *big time* the last week or so, and she was getting worse every day. If she wasn't blasting out his songs at an earsplitting volume like a rebellious teenager, she was planning her outfit and dance moves for the grand unveiling and concert. Mom was completely obsessed. I mean, she was bad enough before, but the prospect of seeing him in the flesh had taken her Switchback fever to a whole new level.

It felt like our roles were reversed—as if she was the kid and I was the grumpy parent nagging her to turn the music down so I could concentrate on my space dragon story. I'd spent all week working on the big intergalactic showdown (trying to, anyway), but the endless Switchback tracks were getting harder and harder to ignore. How was I supposed to write a convincing dragon-laser battle on the planet Scalathon if I couldn't hear myself think? If I couldn't keep Switchback out of my head for five minutes? His lyrics kept creeping into my story when I wasn't looking, turning the evil dragon overlord into a lovestruck lizard.

"Please don't shoot us, Your Gruesome Green Evilness," begged Tailflick, trembling behind his space rock. "We surrender."

"Don't shoot?" roared Fireface, his bulging eyes flashing with anger. "I've been losing my head over you all this time. What will it take to make you mine?"

The worst thing about it was I only had myself to blame. I was the one who'd introduced her to Switchback's songs in the first place. It was my fault she'd turned into Mom the Mega Fan.

"Hey, Mom," I'd made the mistake of saying at the beginning of last summer. "Is it okay if we listen to my new CD in the car?" That was at the start of a ten-hour road trip to visit my cousins.

By the time we got back home, six days later, Mom knew all the words to all the songs and had already ordered a Switchback poster for her office wall. That was the last time I saw my CD too!

Mom had been counting down to Switchback Saturday for what felt like forever, unable to concentrate on anything else. On Monday, she set off to work wearing mismatched shoes. On Tuesday, she packed me off to school with cat food sandwiches. By Wednesday, she was so busy dancing around the house that she forgot to pick me up from football practice, and on Thursday, she tried to make me join in too. She broke off from making dinner to twirl me around the kitchen, oblivious to the shower of peas flying out of the colander in her other hand, and the pork chops burning in the oven.

By Friday, I wasn't sure how much more I could take. But at least she had book club that evening to take her mind off things. At least she'd have her sensible, grown-up girlfriends there to keep her in line. That's what I told myself anyway. *She'll be too busy talking about the book to think about pop stars*, I thought hopefully. *Too busy thinking about plots and characters for any more singing and dancing.* That was before I spotted the book they were going to be discussing—*Switched On to Switchback* by Ivor Crush.

A Switchback book? Seriously? Something told me it was going to be a long night after all.

"I'm so excited for this evening," said Mom, ferrying

bowls of chips into the living room. She was wearing a black Switchback T-shirt and silver-sequined baseball cap (just like the one Switchback wore in his "Tell It to My Broken Heart" video), with too-tight ripped jeans and platform sneakers. She even *looked* like a teenager now. "I've read the book four times already!"

"I hope your friends didn't find it too boring," I said, thinking of Linda the librarian (whose daughter is in my creative writing club) and shy Shianna from the doctor's office. And what about the tall lady who played flute in the local orchestra? What was her name again? Oh yes, Wanda, that was it. I couldn't imagine *her* arm-flapping around the kitchen to Switchback's Greatest Hits. "I mean, it's not the sort of book you usually choose, is it?"

"Boring?" Mom's eyes bulged with disbelief. "*Boring?* How could a book about Switchback be boring? You should try reading it," she said. "I know you've lost interest in him a bit lately, but I still think you'd love it. Especially the chapter about your school. It even mentions Mr. Longdrone!"

Mr. Longdrone, starring in a book about a pop star? Maybe that's what he'd been talking about in morning assembly. I knew it was *something* to do with Switchback, but I drifted off after a bit—off to the planet Scalathon. Mr. Longdrone's assemblies always have that effect on me.

"Speaking of my book club ladies, they'll be here any

moment," said Mom. "Can you take their coats upstairs for me when they arrive?"

"Why? What's wrong with the coat rack?" I asked, turning around to see a big empty space by the front door. "Wait a minute. Where *is* the coat rack?"

"In the garage, waiting for Aunty Lena to collect it tomorrow," said Mom. "It was taking up too much room in the hall—I kept bumping into it when I was practicing my dancing. But it'll be perfect for Lena's new place. She's got a lovely big hallway."

Good for Aunty Lena. "But where are we going to hang our coats?"

Mom shrugged. "I'll put up some hooks this weekend. In the meantime just stick everyone's jackets up in the spare room when they get here for me."

"But I need to work on my story," I said, looking for an excuse to keep out of the way. What if the Switchback book had made all of Mom's friends as bonkers as her? One superfan was bad enough. I wasn't sure I could handle six of them.

"Come on now, Jermy," said Mom, ruffling my hair. I hate it when she calls me that. It makes me sound like I'm infectious. "It won't take you long—just help them with their coats while I finish getting the living room ready. That's all I'm asking. There might even be a piece of cake in it for you."

"Cake? What kind of cake?" How had Mom found time for baking with all that dancing practice?

"Switchback cake, of course," she said, as if that was the only kind there was. "I ordered a special party sponge cake with a photo of his face printed on the icing."

Face cake? Yuck! I wasn't sure I liked the idea of chomping down on the pop star's eyeballs, or licking bits of earlobe off my lips. But maybe I could ask for a slice of the background instead.

"All right," I agreed. "Just as long as you don't start singing."

Chapter 6

Jermaine, 7:32 p.m.

I was wrong about Mom's sensible book club friends. They hadn't found the book boring at all, judging by the overexcited squealing coming from outside.

"Oooeee, Linda! Wow, just look at you. Love, love, LOVE the Switchback sweater. Where did you get it?"

"Oh, I know, it's *gorrrrgeous*, isn't it? My husband had it printed especially for my birthday. Best present EVER! *And* he bought me this special edition of the book—look how shiny it is!"

"Oh my goodness, I want one too. My copy's falling apart because I've read it so many times!"

"Me too, Shianna. I could probably recite most of it by heart!"

Oh great! There was no chance of Mom calming down now. They all sounded as bad as she did.

"Don't just stand there, Jermy," called Mom from the sitting room. "Let them in!"

I forced a smile as I opened the door, mentally preparing myself for a whole evening of Switchback swooning.

"Oh my, Jermaine," said Wanda, tugging off her jacket to reveal a sensible flowered blouse and sweater . . . with a giant light-up I LOVE SB button. "When did you get so tall and grown-up? I hardly recognized you."

She looked different tonight too—I'd never seen her in silver lipstick before. (I didn't even know you could *get* silver lipstick.) And was that glitter on her cheeks?

"You must be so excited about tomorrow," said Linda, handing me her daughter's denim jacket. (I'd recognize that ink stain on the elbow anywhere. She must have borrowed it for the night to try and look cool.) "I know we are, aren't we girls?"

Wanda and Shianna squealed and whooped on cue, waving their books in the air like shakers and wriggling their hips.

Oh help! Is it too late to hide?

Mom let out a matching whoop from the living room.

"Come on through, ladies," she called. "I've got wine and cake—Switchback cake!—and I've shifted all the furniture for some dancing later."

Dancing? I thought this was supposed to be book club, not embarrassing moms dance party!

"Ooo, yes please to dancing," said the short lady with glasses. Was that Marcie? "Unfortunately Gloria and I are double-booked tomorrow, which means we'll miss all the fun. We'll have to make do with a book club boogie tonight instead."

The other women were aghast.

"What? Seriously? Oh gosh, I had no idea."

"Noooooo! I don't believe it!"

"You're kidding me. Oh, I'm so sorry."

Anyone would think something disastrous had happened, the way they were carrying on. Like Marcie's house had been hit by a meteor, or her husband had been kidnapped by aliens.

Marcie shook her head sadly. "I know, I know. But this charity choir concert in Riddlingford Heights has been booked for months, and we promised the conductor we'd be there. They're really short on sopranos at the moment—we can't let them down at such short notice."

"Especially as I'm singing a solo in the second half," piped up Gloria. "They'll *definitely* notice if I'm not there."

"Oh, you poor things," said Mom, looking more serious than

I'd seen her all week. She was doing her sympathetic sad face—the one she wears when someone's died, or when our next-door neighbor pops around to tell us about her cat's diarrhea. "What terrible timing. Come and have some wine and cake. I'll cut you an eyebrow each, how does that sound?"

"Thank you, that sounds wonderful," said Gloria.

"Wonderful," cooed Marcie, like an echo.

Really? I thought, struggling upstairs under a teetering mountain of coats. Eyebrow cake didn't sound particularly wonderful to me. Just hairy.

Chapter 7

Jermaine, 9:10 p.m.

Poor old Switchback didn't last long. When I stuck my head around the door to say good night to Mom, there was only a squashed bit of chin left, with buttercream oozing out the middle.

"I'm off to bed now, Mom," I told her, trying to catch her attention as she shimmied and twirled around the room with Wanda. They were both clutching remote controls, singing into them like pretend microphones, while the ladies on the sofa swayed in time to the music. I guessed the book discussion part of the night was already over.

"Mom!" I tried again, a bit louder. "I'm going to bed now."

I've been losing my head over you all this time, Mom crooned. *What will it ta-ake to ma-ake you mine?*

"MOM!" I yelled. "IT'S BEDTIME!"

"What?" Mom ground to a halt, mid-twirl, staring at me in surprise. "Oh, okay Jermaine. No need to shout. Sleep well."

"Do you think you could keep the music down a bit?" I asked. It was hard enough trying to sleep when Mom had the TV on too loud, let alone a full-on pop concert in the living room.

"Sorry, sweetheart," she said, turning the stereo down low. "I might have gotten a bit carried away there."

Nothing new about that, I thought.

"We'll keep it quiet now, I promise. Sleep well."

"Night, Jermaine," chorused the book club ladies. "Sweet dreams."

Mom was as good as her word when it came to keeping the music down. Apart from a low bass beat pulsing through the bedroom floorboards, I couldn't hear Switchback at all. But I could still hear the ladies, their excited voices drifting up to my bedroom as I lay there trying to get to sleep. They seemed to have moved on from singing and dancing to arguing over who was the biggest Switchback fan.

"I bought his first album the day it came out," boasted someone loudly.

"That was for your daughter though, not you."

"I don't see why that matters. We all used to listen to it together."

"Well I've got every piece of music he's ever recorded. And I live on the same street as his family used to. I get to walk past his old front door every day."

"You're so lucky. I've only just discovered his music since we've been reading this book, but I'm a huge fan now. He's just wonderful. It's such a shame he moved away from Switchington Falls."

"We'll have to grab him tomorrow and stop him from leaving again."

"Ooo yes, that's a good plan, I'm in!"

"Me too!"

"Can we take him back to Riddlingford Heights with us?"

I never got to hear the answer to that last question. The book club chatter drifted into silence as my thoughts grew too heavy to hold on to, my head sinking down into the soft warmth of my pillow. And then my pillow was gone too. I found myself in Polestone Park, dancing alongside Mr. Longdrone, while Switchback sang his latest single to the cheering crowds. They weren't cheering for long though. The singer's microphone (which looked uncannily like our TV remote control) suddenly stopped working, and the sound from the electric guitars fizzled away to nothing. The crowds started booing so loudly that Mr. Longdrone came up onto the stage to tell everyone off.

"That's quite enough of that," said the principal. "Unless you want to be in detention for the rest of the week. I'm sure it's only a temporary hitch. Let's have eyes front, please, and no more talking."

That's when the lights went out. Everyone stopped booing and started screaming instead.

"Book club ladies assemble!" A familiar-sounding voice cut through the chaos. "Linda, you get his arms. Shianna, you're on legs. Wanda? I need you to radio through to Gloria in the getaway car and tell her to start the engine running. Operation Switchback Snatch is GO GO GO!"

"Mom? Is that you?" I called. *What kind of crazy kidnap caper has she gotten herself into?*

"Help!" cried Switchback. "I'm being attacked by book club baddies!"

"Noooooooooo!" came a frantic cry beside me. It was Mishka. "Stop them, Jermaine. Don't let them get away."

"Me?"

"She's your mom," said Mishka. "You have to do something."

Huh! Mishka clearly didn't know my mom very well if she thought *I* could stop her. But she was right—I needed to do *something*. If the police caught the book club crew now, Mom might end up in jail. And then I'd have to go and live with Aunty Lena in her spacious new flat, with only our old coat rack for company. No, I couldn't let that happen. But time was running out. I could already hear sirens wailing in the distance. They were coming for her.

"Hey, Mom," I called, fighting my way through the frightened crowd toward the stage. It seemed lighter now somehow. I could see the book club ladies wrestling the poor pop star into a giant silver I LOVE SWITCHBACK sack, while Mom stood on an armchair giving out instructions. "What about me?" I shouted up to her. "What can I do to help?" I couldn't just stand by and let her get arrested.

Mom grinned. "Jermaine! Boy, am I glad to see you. I need someone to take the coats and make sure there's enough cake to go around."

"But . . ."

"And turn the music up while you're there. I feel a bit of a boogie coming on!"

"But . . ." What were they doing stopping for cake and dancing in the middle of a Switchback snatch?

"Please, Jermy Wermy . . . do it for Mommy."

I woke up in a cold sweat, the crazy kidnap scene still fizzing away in my brain. *Mom! Switchback! The cops!* And then I took in my darkened bedroom and the tangle of bedcovers around my neck and relaxed again. It was just a dream, that was all. Switchback was safe, and Mom wasn't going to jail. The only crimes she'd committed were crimes against fashion, and they couldn't lock her up for that. It all seemed pretty funny now that I was properly awake. I smiled at the idea of the book group ladies bundling poor old Switchback into the back of a van and tearing through town with the police in hot pursuit.

Wait till I tell Mom tomorrow, I thought, imagining the two of us giggling away over breakfast pancakes.

Are you sure that's a good plan? argued a little voice in my head as I yawned and turned over, getting ready to go back to sleep. *You don't want to give her any ideas.*

No, I told the voice. *Mom promised to behave herself tomorrow if I went with her. She promised not to do anything embarrassing.*

And then there were other voices too, drifting up from the living room as I closed my eyes, sinking back into the darkness.

"—can't have you missing out on Switchback—"

"—park nearby for a quick getaway—"

"—mustn't forget the coat rack—"

It sounded like the book club ladies were plotting something. Or maybe I was dreaming again.

Chapter 8

Catalina, Saturday, April 30, 7:30 a.m.

It had been a long, long week, but Saturday was finally here. Not just any old Saturday though. Oh no, this was *Switchback* Saturday.

Switchback, Switchback, Switchback. That's all people had been talking about for days. For weeks. He even got a mention in Friday's assembly! Yes, that's right. Mr. Longdrone talking about pop stars! And as for Mishka . . . well, I know she's my best friend and everything, but that didn't make yesterday's countdown any less annoying. *Twenty-six hours and forty-two minutes until Switchback arrives for the big unveiling . . . Twenty-five hours and thirty-eight minutes until the most exciting event in the history of mankind . . .*

Huh! I could think of a million more exciting things than an ex-pupil of Switchington Falls Middle School pulling an old curtain off some statue. Like Lisa La Loop flying into town to pull an old curtain off a statue instead! That really would be cool.

Don't get me wrong, it wasn't that I didn't *like* Switchback, even though he and Lisa were musical archenemies. He was a pretty good dancer (almost as good as Mishka and me doing our Double Duck dance!), and some of his songs were quite catchy. It wasn't Switchback himself I had a problem with, just the endless, *endless* fuss about his visit. It was the fact that the whole town had turned Switchback crazy in the run-up to the big day.

Switchback, we love you. Switchback, you're amazing. Switchback, Switchback, Switchback!

And the fact that Mishka kept checking her watch every three minutes to see how much time had passed since the last time she checked—that was pretty annoying too. *What time is it now? Oh my goodness, oh my goodness. That means it's only six squillion more seconds until he gets here.*

I had my own countdown going too by the end. Counting

down to school dismissal, that was. Counting down until I could forget about The Most Exciting Event in The Entire History of Switchington Falls for five whole minutes. But now the big day was finally here, and it was only a matter of time before Switchback fever caught up with me all over again.

"Morning, Cat," said Mom, poking her head around my bedroom door.

"Hwwhhwh?" I mumbled, doing my best to stay asleep, trying to get back into the crazy dream I'd been having. No, it was no good—the spell was well and truly broken.

Mom sounded super-bright and cheerful. "I was just saying 'good morning,' that's all. Sorry, sweetheart, I thought you were already awake—I could have sworn I heard you singing. Something about socks, it sounded like. You must have been doing it in your sleep."

Yes, I *had* been singing about socks—I remembered that—and I wished I still was. It had been one of the best dreams ever. But I was awake now, whether I liked it or not.

"Socks and ties," I agreed, rubbing my eyes. I sat up and checked my bedside clock. Half past seven? Huh? Mom didn't usually get up until ten o'clock after her Friday late shift. What was going on?

"All ready for Switchback's visit?" asked Mom, beaming from ear to ear. "Only four and a half hours until he gets here!"

What? Oh no. Not Mom as well. Is there no *escape from The Great Concert Countdown?*

"I'm just heading out to the hair salon for my cut and color," said Mom. "They've opened up extra early today to fit everyone in before the big performance."

"You mean you're going to see it too? I thought you preferred old music, like the Beatles. And Mozart."

Mom pulled a face. "You make me sound like a dinosaur! Besides, *everyone's* going. Even great grandma. Dad's promised her a nice space at the back in case she needs to sit down."

Great grandma? I couldn't imagine her twirling her hips to "Losing My Head Over You." More like "Losing My False Teeth Over You."

"Don't worry. I know you don't want to be dancing in the back with us oldies," said Mom. "That's why I've arranged for you to go with Mishka. Dad says he'll drop you off at her house after figure skating and you can get ready together." She tilted her head to one side, watching me carefully. "You could look a *little* more pleased. I realize Switchback's not your favorite, but he's very good live, you know."

I tried to look more enthusiastic, wondering when Mom had become such an expert on pop music.

"One of the men from work saw him on tour last year with his daughters," Mom went on. "He was brilliant, apparently."

"Not as good as Lisa La Loop, I bet. Why can't we go and see *her* live instead?"

"Because, Miss Grumpalina, she's not the one opening the new performance hall, is she?" Mom lifted up the end of the duvet and tickled my feet to cheer me up. "You'll have a fantastic time once you get there," she promised. "Trust me."

I knew she was right, really. I knew I'd be singing and dancing along with everyone else once the music started. And a free concert right on our doorstep was too good an opportunity to pass up. But I still wished it was Lisa La Loop who'd gone to our school, just like in my dream last night. I could still remember it all, as clear as day.

I dreamt she'd joined our class—as a fully grown adult!—and I got to be her partner during music. For some reason Mr. Longdrone was in charge of the lesson, teaching us a boring song about neckties to prepare for the opening ceremony at the new performance hall.

"All right. Back to the chorus, everyone," he said, using the end of his own tie as a conductor's baton. "All together now . . ."

We all droned, *Don't forget to knot it tight,*

It helps your tie to stay,

Or try my special Velcro one

In seven shades of gray.

Mr. Longdrone let out a long satisfied sigh. "Now *that's* what I call music. Let's just hope young Switchback learns those extra verses I sent him in time. The audience will be expecting to hear all forty-two."

Switchback was going to be singing the tie song at the opening ceremony? All forty-two verses? Even in the weird world of dreams, that still seemed like an odd idea.

"And now I'd like you all to split up into pairs and work on some verses of your own," said Mr. Longdrone. "Just in case Switchback needs any more for his encore."

The rest of the class groaned, but I was so pleased to be working with Lisa I didn't care *what* we were writing.

"Ties, huh?" she said, pulling a full-size electric guitar out of her pencil case. "That sounds a bit dull, doesn't it?"

I nodded, too starstruck to speak.

"How about we mix it up a bit then?" she suggested. "What do you say?"

Another nod.

"Any ideas?" She looked at me expectantly.

My dream brain went into panic mode. I was too busy thinking *Look at me, I'm sitting here with Lisa La Loop* to come up with anything intelligent.

Come on, Catalina, think! Think of something fun and cool. Something wild and exciting . . . Nail-clippers? Toothpicks? Glasses wipes? "S-s-socks?" I stammered at last.

"Socks? Really?" Lisa looked surprised. "Something like this, you mean?" She picked up her electric guitar and broke out into a totally amazing song about losing her favorite sock in the clothes dryer.

And if you all liked my sick song
About some old odd socks, she finished,
You'll love this one by my friend Cat,
Her awesome sock song rocks.

And then suddenly I had an electric guitar too, and I was

warbling away like the world's second-best sock-song singer ever. We'd just moved on to a duet version of my all-time favorite Lisa La Loop hit, "I'll Be Your Coat Rack," when Mr. Longdrone called for the final bell and I woke up back in my bed to find Mom grinning in the doorway. She was still grinning now, even as she stood there telling me how much it would mean to Mishka to have me at the concert today. How it wasn't Mishka's fault that it was Switchback coming instead of Lisa La Loop.

Yes, I thought, feeling bad for getting so grumpy about the constant countdown the day before. Mishka was just excited, that was all. Seeing Switchback was like a dream come true. I should be excited for her, just like she'd be excited for me if it was Lisa La Loop coming to Switchington to sing about socks. I pasted on a matching grin of my own and climbed out of bed, ready to face the day. *Switchback, here we come. Four hours, twenty-five minutes, and counting.*

Chapter 9

Catalina, 10:30 a.m.

I really *was* excited by the time I finished ice-skating. I was pepped up on music, adrenaline, and an extra-large caramel cashew energy bar. It was turning into a good day after all.

I'd been struggling with the same routine for weeks, losing my timing just before the double jump and ending up on the wrong foot. But today was the breakthrough I'd been waiting for. Instead of changing the jump, Coach had decided to change the music instead, swapping "Random Orchestral Ice-Skating Track" by Some Old Guy for "I'll Be Your Coat Rack," by Lisa La Loop.

"I heard it on the radio during the week," he'd told me, jiggling his hips in time to the catchy beat, "and thought it would be perfect."

He'd been right, of course. It *was* perfect. All of it was perfect. Perfect music, perfect routine, and a perfect double jump on my very first attempt. It must have been the song working its magic, powering through my legs like an ice-dancing dream.

"That was brilliant," said Dad as we walked back to the car, chomping on our caramel cashew energy bars. (The most energetic thing Dad ever does at the rink is read the newspaper, but he's a sucker for caramel cashews.) "I don't think I've ever seen you skate as well as that."

"It's all down to Lisa," I told him, reliving the jumps in my head as I took another big bite of the bar.

Dad nodded. "Lisa Smith from school, you mean? Has she been giving you tips?"

"No. Lisa La Loop," I mumbled through a mouthful of sticky, nutty deliciousness. That clearly wasn't the answer he was expecting, judging by the look on his face.

"Lisa's a poop? That's not very nice. I thought she was one of your friends."

What?! I could hardly swallow for giggling.

"No," I finally managed. "Lisa La Loop. You know, my favorite singer ever—the one whose song I was skating to today."

Except it turned out Dad *didn't* know about Lisa, after all. "I thought you liked Jamster Hamster and the Sweet Squeaks?"

"They *used* to be my favorite," I admitted. "When I was five. But Lisa La Loop's way cooler than a singing hamster."

"What about this Switchback fellow everyone keeps going on about?" asked Dad. "The one Mom's dragging me to see later? I thought *he* was supposed to be the coolest singer around?"

I snorted. "Huh! Lisa's *ten* times cooler than him. A hundred times cooler, in fact. She even makes odd socks sound exciting," I boasted, forgetting for a moment that was only in my dream.

"Really? I bet she's not as cool as me though," said Dad, breaking into an embarrassing dad dance in the middle of the parking lot. "I bet she can't bus moves like this."

"No one *buses* moves," I pointed out, as a fresh round of giggles bubbled up inside. I was trying not to laugh—trying not to encourage him—but it *was* funny. "It's *bust* a move."

"That's what you think. How's this for a bus move?" Dad dropped down into a low squat, turning his hands on an invisible steering wheel. An entire bus full of Girl Scouts had their heads pressed to the windows, watching him. "Next stop, Cool Avenue, Coolsville."

"S-s-stop it," I spluttered, giggling so hard it hurt. "S-s-someone might see."

"Ah yes, good point," said Dad, straightening back up again. "I don't want anyone copying my signature moves before the concert today. Got to keep my dance material fresh for the fans."

I was 99 percent certain he was joking. But what if he wasn't? What if Dad really *was* planning on unleashing "The Bus" on the people of Switchington Falls? Thank goodness I was going with Mishka!

"I'd better save my voice too," he added, "to prep for my big duet with Switchback. Did I tell you he's invited me to sing with him onstage?"

I was 100 percent sure he was joking this time. Dad's singing talents made "The Bus" seem like the work of a dancing superstar. Imagine a tone-deaf cat with a cold . . . no, a cat's putting it too kindly. Imagine a tone-deaf coyote with a splinter in its paw—an entire pack of coyotes, actually, with injured paws and chili juice in their eyes. *That's* what Dad sounded like when he sang. Signing him up for a duet would be a really mean trick to play on everyone.

And that's when it hit me. *Mean tricks! Of course!* I almost dropped my energy nut bar in excitement. Why hadn't I thought of it before?

"Are you all right?" asked Dad as we reached the car. "You're looking very flushed all of a sudden."

I was better than all right. I felt brilliant! I'd just remembered the prank Switchback played on Lisa La Loop at her last big concert. He hired a plane to fly over the stadium and spell out his name in red smoke as the fans arrived. The newspapers said it was revenge for the trick Lisa played on him at the end of his Florida tour, when a giant I LOVE LISA LA LOOP helium balloon came bobbing out across the stage halfway through his opening number. Mishka wasn't very impressed when she saw the pictures on her Switchback fan feed, but Lisa was just getting her own back for the skating squirrel stunt Switchback had pulled at the International Music Awards the month before. Their rivalry had become almost as famous as them, with each payback trick bigger and bolder than the one before. It was good news for record sales, and good news for me too, hopefully. Where better for Lisa to prank Switchback than his old hometown?

"I'm fine," I told Dad, stuffing the rest of my nut bar into my sweatpants pocket, too excited to manage any more. "I've had a bit of an idea, that's all." A brilliant, breathtaking, best-day-ever burst of inspiration.

Dad winked. "Let me guess, you want to borrow my bus move to impress all your friends at the concert today?"

"It's certainly tempting," I joked, "but Mishka and I already have our own dance, thanks—the Double Duck. No, I was just thinking Lisa might be in town today too, planning her latest trick on Switchback." The idea sent shivers down my spine. "I might even get to meet her!" It would be just like in my dream—the two of us together—only without the socks this time.

"The famously cool Lisa the Poop? That *is* exciting," said Dad. "Perhaps she'll be more interested in my bus move, seeing as she's so cool. I bet that's the real reason she's in town, isn't it? She's come to take lessons from the King of Cool himself." He patted his chest and winked again. "Don't worry, Miss Poop," he called across the parking lot in an embarrassingly loud voice. "We're on our way."

Chapter 10

Catalina, 11:30 a.m.

We were still on our way nearly an hour later, stuck in the worst traffic jam Switchington Falls had ever seen. It would have been quicker to walk.

"Word must have gotten out about my duet with Switchback," joked Dad. "That's why the roads are so busy."

"Hmm," I said, too busy watching the clock on the dash to play along. What if we didn't get there in time? What if I missed my chance to see Lisa? The longer we sat in traffic—a never-ending line of stationary cars and trucks—the more convinced I was that she'd put in an appearance.

Yes, today was the day. I could feel it in my bones. While we were going nowhere fast in a horn-beeping haze of diesel fumes, my musical hero was probably already in town, preparing to unleash the best pop-star payback ever. I wasn't sure what that payback would be, exactly, but I knew it would be something big and bold and brilliant. Maybe she'd parachute in over Polestone Park with a giant banner that said "Lisa La Loop is Number One." Or perhaps she'd burst her way out of a special "Welcome to Switchington Falls" cake and surprise everyone. A bungee jump out of a helicopter, halfway through "Losing My Head Over You"? That would be totally awesome. Or . . . or . . . maybe she'd clamber out of a big black van in the bus station parking lot, talking to someone on her cell phone . . .

"It's her!" I shrieked, pointing out the passenger window as the traffic finally—finally!—started to move again.

"What?" asked Dad. "Who? Where?" He restarted the engine as the car behind us honked its horn.

"Lisa La Loop," I cried, my heart beating like crazy. I was right! "Over there by that van," I said, tapping on the glass, "with dark glasses and a big hat tucked under her arm. It looks like she's—"

"What?" asked Dad again, sounding flustered. "I can't hear

with all this racket." There was a whole chorus of beeps behind us now. "All right, all right, I'm going," he said, addressing his rearview mirror. "Honestly, talk about impatient."

"Wait!" I shrieked, as we rolled straight past the van. Straight past Lisa. "Stop. Slow down!"

Dad was completely flustered now. "What? What is it? What's wrong?"

"It's Lisa. She's here. We have to stop."

"I can't really stop here, honey. Not with all this traffic."

"But we have to turn around. I need to see her. I need to . . ." It *was* her. I knew it was. But by now she was just a dark shape in the mirror.

"Sorry," said Dad as the Lisa La Loop shape disappeared altogether. "We're stuck in this lane now whether we like it or not. And we don't want to keep Mishka waiting any longer—she'll be getting worried."

Oh yes, Mishka. Judging by the twenty-two "WHERE ARE YOU?" texts I'd received from her in the last ten minutes (all in capital letters, with more question marks added every time), she was way past worried. Full-on panic was more like it.

My phone pinged again, right on cue.

"WHERE ARE YOU??????????????????????????????????"

Oh dear, there must have been thirty question marks this

time—she was getting desperate. Dad was right. It wasn't fair to keep her waiting any longer.

"Be there in five minutes," I texted back, my heart sinking all the way down to my sneakers at the thought of leaving Lisa behind. I'd just have to hope for a good view when she parachuted in later, or did whatever amazing stunt she had planned.

Mishka was already waiting outside when we got to her house, dressed in her hand-painted I ❤ SWITCHBACK T-shirt and hopping from foot to foot with impatience.

"Sorry we're so late," Dad called out the window. "The traffic was all kinds of crazy coming back into town. You girls have fun now," he added as I scrambled out of the car. "If you see Switchback, tell him I'm on my way. Tell him I'm looking forward to our duet later." He wasn't giving up on that joke, was he? "And don't forget the bus move if you want to impress your friends!"

I only wished I *could* forget it. "Promise me you won't do that in public today," I begged. "I'm not sure the world's quite ready for *that* level of cool."

"At last!" said Mishka, as Dad drove off, still chuckling to himself. "I thought you'd *never* get here." She let out a high-pitched shriek as she checked her watch. "Oh my goodness, oh my goodness. It's only twenty-three minutes and seventeen seconds until he arrives. We need to get going NOW! Dad!" she yelled, running back to the house to fetch her father. "Cat's here. It's time to go."

Mr. Patel didn't look nearly as excited about Switchback's arrival as his daughter. "I still don't know why Mom couldn't take you," he grumbled as Mishka dragged him down the path. "Of all the weekends to have to work."

"Please, Dad, hurry up," said Mishka. "Otherwise we'll be stuck at the back and won't be able to see anything. Come on, less talking, more walking."

"Hey, guess who I saw on the way back from practice?" I asked, as Mishka speed-marched us along the sidewalk.

"Switchback?" Her eyes lit up like candles on a cake. "Oh my goodness, oh my goodness, I can't believe he's here already."

"No, not Switchback."

The lights in Mishka's eyes blew out again, her face furrowing into a frown. "It wasn't the Meaner Lisa gang, was it?"

"The who?" I didn't have a clue what she was talking about.

"The Who?" Mr. Patel cut in, before Mishka could answer. "You mean that British rock band from the 1960s? The ones who sang 'Pinball Wizard'? I didn't realize they were playing today as well."

"No. Not the Who. Lisa La Loop!" I waited for their gasps of amazement, but they never came.

"Oh," said Mr. Patel, sounding disappointed. "That's a shame. I like the Who."

"Oh," said Mishka, like an echo. "She's probably planning some silly stunt to ruin our big day. I hope the police are ready for her."

"The Police, did you say?" asked Mr. Patel. "You mean that British band from the 1970s and '80s? The ones who sang 'Every Breath You Take'? Are they playing today as well?"

"Seriously, Dad," said Mishka. "We haven't got time for this. Let's just concentrate on getting to the park, shall we? Getting ready for Switchback. The ONE AND ONLY performer who's going to be there today. Okay?"

"And Lisa La Loop," I added under my breath, keeping my eyes peeled for black vans and women in wide-brimmed hats, scanning the sky for planes and parachutes, for helicopters and hot-air balloons. Whatever stunt she was planning, it was going to be a good one. I just knew it.

Chapter 11

Kai, Saturday, April 30, 9:15 a.m.

"This promises to be a *very* exciting day for the residents of Switchington Falls," said the lady on the radio, "thanks to a visit from music megastar Switchback, who'll be opening the town's new music venue at a special ceremony later today."

"Wow," said the other presenter. "I can only imagine how excited the folk of Switchington must be right now."

I didn't need to imagine it. I could tell just by glancing around the room. The only person who seemed remotely excited was Luli, my little sister, who bounced up and down in her seat like a fidgety frog. Everyone else looked bored or nervous, or, in old Mrs. Mothgrot's case, just plain miserable. To be fair, there were more exciting places to be waiting for Switchback's arrival than the dentist's office, and Mrs. Mothgrot *always* looked miserable.

"That's us!" shrieked Luli, nudging me in the ribs with her comic. "They're talking about us on the radio!"

Excitement was spilling off her in waves now—wriggly, jiggly waves of can't-sit-still excitement at the thought of all her favorite things crammed into one day. Luli loved Switchback (you should hear her singing along to the car radio at the top of her voice), *and* she loved trips to the dentist. She loved the comics Mom bought us to read in the waiting room (*Super Math Girl* for Luli and *Zombie Zac* for me), and she loved going up and down on the big black dentist chair. Anyone would think it was a fairground ride to hear her squealing and giggling. She even loved those stickers the dental assistant gave out for having nice clean teeth, and she refused to let Mom wash her clothes until the sticker had worn away. I'd given Luli mine as well today (we'd already had our appointments; we were just waiting for Dad to finish with the hygienist), so she had one on her sweater and one on her forehead, which looked a bit weird. She'd probably refuse to wash her face now until that one wore off too.

"Did you hear it?" she asked, nudging me in the chest with the sharp end of *Super Math Girl*. "Did you hear what they said?"

I nodded. Yes, I'd heard. But I had better things to think about than Switchback—like whether Zac would escape from the evil school janitor in "Zac and the Broom Closet of Doom" or not. The comic stories were even more gripping than the *Zombie Zac* TV show.

"It's less than three hours till he gets here now," said Luli. "I wonder what he'll be wearing today? The silver suit or the gold one?"

"Who knows," I said, not really minding either way. *Come on, Zac, you'll have to stagger faster than that.* It was no good though. No matter how many bowls of Brain Flakes Zac ate for breakfast, he was still no match for the fiendish janitor and his turbocharged vacuum cleaner. I was just hoping he had a cunning plan up his sleeve. Or what was left of his sleeve, anyway. (Zac's Bartford Brain Academy uniform looked like it had battled with a few killer washing machines in its time—and lost.)

"Do you think he'll do his special Switchback dance?" asked Luli. "The one with the robot arms and wriggly snake bottom?"

"Hmm," I grunted. *Oh no. Not the demon duster! Come on. Think, Zac, think!*

"You're not even listening to me, are you?" Luli was starting to sound cross now.

"What? Yes, of course I am. Only . . ." Only Zac had just had a brainwave. *The secret tunnel under the science tower? Nice one! There's no way the janitor will be able to squeeze in there after him.*

"What if I told you Mrs. Mothgrot just got beamed up by aliens?" asked Luli, trying to catch me out.

"Really? That's good," I murmured. To be honest, I didn't think anyone would miss her if she got zapped into outer space.

"And the fish in the fish tank just bit the receptionist's finger off," said Luli.

Uh-oh. The janitor might be too big to squeeze into the tunnel, but the extra-long nozzle on his vicious vacuum isn't.

"Two fingers, in fact," Luli continued. "I think they must be piranhas."

"Probably," I said, even though there's no way piranhas would fit in such a tiny tank as that. *Come on, Zac, can't you crawl any quicker?*

Luli was quiet for a bit, leaving me to read in peace. But not for long. "And a real-life zombie just came out of Dr. Ling's room."

"Good one," I said, getting to the bottom of the page to find one of those "To Be Continued . . ." signs. *No! You can't just leave the story there! I need to know what happens.*

"I'm not joking this time," Luli hissed. "Look!" She nudged me again, harder than ever.

"Yes, yes, very funny," I said, finally looking up from my comic to find a real-life zombie leaning against the reception desk.

What??? I blinked once . . . twice . . . three times, but it didn't make any difference. He was still there.

"But that's . . ." My brain kept telling me it was impossible—a zombie at the dentist's? In Switchington Falls?—but he was every bit as real as Luli wriggling beside me. As real as Mom, checking her watch and wondering when Dad would be finished. As real as Mrs. Mothgrot, glaring at the magazine she was reading and tutting under her breath. As real as me. He had his credit card clenched tight in his fist, and the other hand pressed against his jaw, as if his teeth still hurt from whatever Dr. Ling had been doing to them.

"But that's . . ." *That's what? Awesome? Crazy? Cool? Ten types of terrifying?* It was kind of scary and exciting all at the same time.

I looked around the waiting room, waiting for the full zombie apocalypse panic to kick in, but no one else seemed to have noticed. What about the receptionist, though? Why wasn't she cowering behind her desk at the sight of his hideous undead face and peeled-off green skin? Why wasn't she screaming for someone to fetch a Zombie Blaster 500, like the one the substitute Spanish teacher threatens Zac with in season two, episode seven, instead of smiling sweetly and asking him if he felt better now?

The zombie nodded. "Mush bether now, thanz," he mumbled,

as if his mouth was too swollen to talk properly. Huh! Too full of dentist brains, more like. Poor Dr. Ling. "Thanz for fithing me in tho wickly."

"You're welcome, Mr. Dearlove," said the receptionist, still smiling as she handed him his bill.

Mr. Dearlove? What kind of a scary zombie name is that?

"We couldn't have you missing the big show today, could we?" she asked, passing the card reader over to him.

"No," said the zombie, punching in his pin code with his gruesome undead fingers. "I've been waithing a long thime for this."

Waiting a long time for what? For a moment I thought he must be a Switchback fan too, dragging himself back out of the grave for a glimpse of his musical hero—for the chance to dance along to his favorite tracks. But then it hit me. He didn't want to *watch* Switchback at all, did he? No, he wanted to *eat* him. He didn't care about Switchback's amazing voice, just his tasty brain . . .

"We should tell someone," I whispered to Luli. "Before it's too late." It wouldn't matter *what* color suit Switchback was wearing for his performance if he didn't have a brain anymore.

"I thought you *liked* zombies," she said. "I thought you said Zombie Zac was a hundred times cooler than Super Math Girl. A *thousand* times cooler."

I had said that, yes, but only because Luli was wrestling

the remote control off me at the time, trying to switch channels halfway through my favorite episode ever. Talk about annoying! And besides, Zombie Zac was a *nice* zombie—that's what made the show so fun. He was more interested in improving his own brains than gobbling up other people's, more interested in *meeting* new friends than *eating* them. He wasn't even especially horrible to look at (apart from that episode where his left eyeball kept popping out, which was kind of gross).

But *this* zombie was nothing like Zac. He was twice the size for a start, and his face looked like something out of a horror movie. (Not that I've ever watched a horror movie—Mom says I'm not old enough—but I've seen the posters up outside the movie theater.) Oh yes, and this zombie was real—that was the other difference. A rather *big* difference. I couldn't believe everyone was just sitting there with a real-life (or should that be real-dead?) brain eater on the loose. I couldn't believe no one had noticed—not even the receptionist. Maybe she was color-blind and couldn't see his green skin. Maybe she needed glasses. Or maybe she was just playing it cool, reaching for a special attack-of-the-undead panic button under her desk, even as she sat there smiling back at him. But it would be too late by the time the police got here. He'd be long gone by then, already tucking into poor old Switchback.

"Mom," I hissed. "There's a zombie in the waiting room.

What should we do?" *Zap him with a dentist drill? Strap him to a chair with dental floss?*

"That's nice, dear," said Mom, her face buried in her magazine.

"*Seriously.* A big ugly zombie looking for fresh brains to eat." He didn't seem interested in *our* brains, luckily. Maybe he was taking a rest after Dr. Ling, saving some room for his musical main course at midday.

"Mmm," said Mom. "That looks like a nice recipe. Chicken and red pepper bake. Maybe we could try that tonight?"

"And now he's getting away," I said, watching as undead Mr. Dearlove headed toward the door.

"Although I *was* thinking of doing cauliflower and cheese . . ."

My stomach turned. *I* was thinking of baked brains sitting in a dish of gooey yellow ooze . . . And then suddenly I wasn't thinking at all. I was up on my feet, running out the door after the disappearing zombie before *my* brain had a chance to stop me.

"Be careful, Kai," called Luli, chasing after me. "He might be dangerous."

"I will," I promised. There's no way I was tackling the undead Mr. Dearlove on my own. Not without a Zombie Blaster 500. "Don't worry, I'll be back before you know it. I just want to see which way he goes—find out what he's planning. If Mom asks where I've gone, tell her . . . tell her I had a headache. Tell her

I popped out for some fresh air." *And if I'm not back in the next half hour, tell her to ring the Supernatural Swat Squad!*

I didn't like lying, but the truth would be too much for Mom to handle (if she even believed it). Besides, the thought of zombies loose in the town was enough to give *anyone* a headache. And if my suspicions were right, a pretend sore head was nothing compared to the skull-splitting one waiting for Switchback when he arrived at the performance hall.

Chapter 12

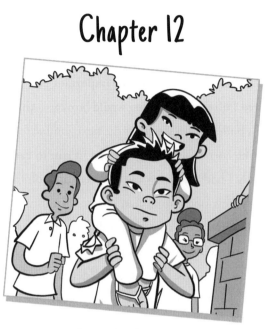

Kai, 9:30 a.m.

Mr. Dearlove was surprisingly sprightly for a member of the walking dead. (That's what they call zombies in films, I think. That's what it said on Zombie Zac's latest report card too, under "Extracurricular clubs and societies": *Fortunately, being a member of the walking dead has not interfered with Zac's membership in the school table tennis society this year, although the unfortunate mix-up with the bouncing eyeball did cause some confusion during the inter-school finals.*)

"Super-speedy, long-legged striding dead" would have been a more accurate description, I decided, watching Mr. Dearlove tear off down the road. But I guess that's not quite as catchy. *Help! The super-speedy, long-legged striding dead are coming!*

He was fast, anyway; that's the important part. By the time I'd reassured Luli that everything would be okay—that I wouldn't end up as a boiled brain starter at the next zombie feast—he was almost at the corner already, and I had to run to catch up with him. Luckily I had my trusty old sneakers on, holes and all, not the squeaky new ones Mom had ordered for me. Any passing zombies would hear me coming a mile away in them.

The street seemed oddly empty for a Saturday morning—everyone else must have been at home, getting ready for the big lunchtime performance. Or maybe they were already down at Polestone Park, lining up for a good spot. On the one hand, that was a good thing—it meant there were fewer juicy brains to tempt Mr. Dearlove with—but on the other hand, it meant there was no one else around to stop him. No one who could help if he suddenly turned on *me*. When it came to tracking a dangerous zombie through the streets of Switchington Falls, it looked like I was on my own.

I followed behind at a safe distance—at least I *hoped* it was safe—ducking into shop doorways to hide whenever he looked like he was slowing down. But then the shops ran out, and we

were on the open road heading for the abandoned dance academy on the outskirts of town. There were no handy doorways to duck into out here. If he happened to turn around now, looking for his next meal, I'd be a goner.

It's funny, but I'd never thought of zombies as being particularly clever before. I mean, when was the last time you saw a reanimated corpse scoop the jackpot on *Who Wants to Be a Millionaire?* (They'd probably do better on *Who Wants to Eat a Millionaire?*) But maybe I was wrong. Maybe a daily diet of brains made *them* brainy too. Mr. Dearlove certainly seemed to know what he was doing. No one ever went to the dance academy anymore, not since the old lady who ran it died a few years back. Some kids even said it was haunted, which was enough to keep anyone away. That made it the perfect place for a zombie to lay low while he waited for his next meal—a nice juicy Switchback Sandwich?—to arrive. *Cunning. Very cunning.*

I checked my watch. Dad's appointment with the hygienist would be over soon. If I wasn't back by then, he and Mom would start to worry. In fact, Mom might be worrying already if she'd finished her magazine and noticed I was gone. She could be scouring the streets at that very moment, looking for her poor, headachy son.

Exactly, said the sensible part of my brain. *Turn around now, before you get into trouble. Before you end up as a post-dentist zombie snack. Go back and tell the police what you've seen and let them deal with Mr. Dearlove. Or the army. Either way, this is a job for professionals.*

But don't you want to see where he goes? What he does? asked the not-so-sensible part of my brain. The wild, adventurous part that thought the arrival of a zombie was the most exciting thing that had ever happened in Switchington Falls. The part that secretly wanted to save the day, like some kind of super-action hero, and be awarded a "Services to Zombie Combat" certificate of achievement from Mr. Longdrone at a special school assembly.

There'll be no certificates if that zombie catches you, warned Boring Brain. *And the only assembly speech Mr. Longdrone will be giving is your memorial one. Followed by an extra-long lecture about the dangers of tackling strange monsters, because* all *his lectures are extra long.*

You don't have to fight him to be a hero, said Adventurous Brain. *Just find out what he's up to and let the police and the military take it from there. But they'll need to know if he's working alone or if there's a whole zombie army preparing to invade.*

Okay, okay. Five more minutes, tops, and then you turn around, agreed my sensible side, sensing it was beaten. *But stick to the shadows, and don't let him see you.*

Keeping to the shadows was easier said than done, though, as we turned off the road and cut across the old dance academy parking lot. There weren't many shadows around, given how empty the place was. An abandoned shopping cart sat rusting away in one corner, with a surprisingly new-looking minibus parked in the other—goodness knew what *that* was doing there—but other than that, the place was deserted. Just a few sparrows pecking around. And me. Oh yes, and a man-eating zombie looking for a nice, quiet place to digest his breakfast dentist.

It was certainly quiet, all right. No one would hear me screaming all the way out here, I realized with a shiver. I should have borrowed Mom's cell phone so I could call for help if things got sticky. I could have taken photos then too, to prove I was telling the truth. What if the police laughed in my face when I told them what I'd discovered?

A flesh-eating zombie? Ha, ha. Very funny. It's not Halloween for another half a year, you know.

I wouldn't blame them if they did, either. *I* wouldn't have believed there was a zombie on the loose in sleepy old Switchington Falls if I hadn't seen it with my own eyes. But it was too late to worry about phones now. By the time I got back to the dentist's waiting room, it would be time to go home.

I left a good safe distance between us as I trailed the zombie toward the main building, hardly daring to breathe in case he turned around and spotted me.

Don't even think *about going in there after him,* ordered the sensible part of my brain. *You'll never come out alive.*

I'm not going in. Just a quick peek through the door, that's all. I just want to see what he's up to. I just want to know why there's music coming from inside.

But when I got there, the door was jammed open like an invitation, and I followed Mr. Dearlove inside without stopping to think. Crazy theories jostled for my attention as I crept through the abandoned entrance toward the main hall, the music growing louder with every step. Maybe the old dance academy was more than just a place to lay low? Maybe Mr. Dearlove was planning on doing some ballet practice while he was there—unknotting the dead muscles in his legs with some bends and stretches at the barre? (Like in "Zombie Zac and the Terrible Tutu," where the school football coach decided the players needed ballet lessons to help with their strength and coordination—I loved that episode.) Or a nice bit of zombie tap dancing to help with his digestion? Perhaps he was training for *Dancing with the Undead Stars* or *America's Got Zombie Talent*? That really *would* be crazy. Or would it?

By the time I reached the hall doors, the music was louder than ever, with low bass vibrations running all the way through the floor to my feet. Loud music was good, though—the louder the better, in fact. It covered up the sound of my heart thumping inside my chest as I peered through the glass panel in one of the doors. It covered up the high-pitched squeal of shock that came bursting out of my mouth when I saw what was happening inside.

Chapter 13

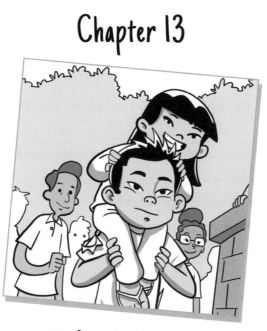

Kai, 9:45 a.m.

One zombie was bad enough. Two would have been double trouble. But the sight of an entire gang of zombies limbering up in the middle of the dance hall had me shaking like a cat on a washing machine.

The tallest, greenest, scariest-looking one of the lot slapped Mr. Dearlove on the shoulder as if he was welcoming him back to the gang. The music was too loud to hear what they were saying, though—I could only guess.

There you are! How was the dentist?

Deee-licious, with a lovely aftertaste of mint. I didn't get a sticker though.

And no one saw you come back here afterward? No one tried to follow you?

Nope. Our top-secret hideout and zombie dance hall is as secret as ever.

Good. Otherwise we'd have had to eat them too, and then there'd be less time for dancing.

One of the others clapped his hands—*Places everybody!*—and the zombies formed two lines of six in the middle of the hall. Two lines of foot-tapping, hip-swaying zombies, all nodding their heads in time to the music. It was a surprisingly catchy tune, with a deep guitar and drum bass line and a snazzy keyboard intro that was made for dancing. Not that I was doing any dancing, of course—I was too busy watching them. Too busy trembling. Up came their arms, stretching out in front of them as they staggered forward like, well, like zombies, really. That's when the bloodthirsty chanting began. Not even the music could drown *that* out.

"Switch-back, Switch-back, we want Switch-back," they groaned in unison, like the world's scariest fans ever.

I was right! Poor old Dr. Ling the dentist had only been an appetizer. And now Mr. Dearlove and his gruesome crew were

holding out for the music megastar main course! Someone needed to warn Switchback before it was too late. And it looked like that someone was me.

I crept back out of the building as quietly as I could, back into the bright morning sunshine. And then I ran, tearing across the parking lot like a rocket-fueled roadrunner, sprinting across the weed-strewn asphalt as if my life depended on it—which it probably did. If those zombies caught me now, I was done for.

Faster, faster, said the panicked voice in my head as I hurtled back along the road to town, imagining long zombie legs chasing after me. Imagining the new chant they'd be singing as their outstretched zombie arms lumbered toward me. *Kai, Kai, we want Kai . . .*

I didn't stop to listen though. Didn't stop to look. I pushed on faster than ever, careening past the shops toward the dentist's office at a gazillion miles an hour. Straight into the outstretched arms of a red-eyed, angry-looking . . .

Mom.

Thank goodness!

"Kai!" cried Mom, hugging me tight into her chest as if I'd been gone for days. Weeks. Maybe she wasn't angry after all. Just worried. "Where were you? Luli said you'd popped out for some fresh air, but we couldn't find you anywhere."

"I told them about the zombie too, but they didn't believe me," piped up a little voice. That's when I noticed Luli and Dad standing nearby.

"I . . . I . . . was at the . . . old dance . . . academy," I panted, trying to catch my breath. "That's where the . . . zombies are. Lots . . . of zombies."

"The dance academy?" asked Mom, ignoring the bit about the zombies. "But that's blocks away from here. You can't just run off without telling anyone where you're going, Kai."

"I'm sorry," I said, wriggling out of her grasp. "But I had to see . . . what they were up to . . . I think one of them ate Dr. Ling!"

Luli giggled.

"I can assure you no one's eaten Dr. Ling," said Dad. "We just saw him talking to the receptionist."

Really? Thank goodness for that. "But the zombie—Mr. Dearlove—Luli saw him too. What was he doing in Dr. Ling's room if he wasn't there for breakfast?"

"Perhaps he had a toothache?" Luli suggested. "That's why he had his hand over his mouth when he came out."

"I guess . . . But that doesn't mean he's not dangerous," I insisted. Why wasn't anyone taking the zombie invasion seriously? "We still need to go to the police. We need to get a message to Switchback before it's too late. I heard them chanting his name."

Mom shook her head. "The only place *you're* going is home. I don't know what's gotten into you today, running off like that and filling your sister's head with nonsense about zombies. Consider yourself lucky you're not grounded," she said sternly. "But that wouldn't be fair to Luli. She's been looking forward to seeing Switchback for weeks, and Dad and I promised we'd take Grandma out for lunch today."

"It's not nonsense." If only Mom had looked up from her magazine when I first spotted Mr. Dearlove. Then she'd *know* I was telling the truth. "There really *was* a zombie—ask the receptionist if you don't believe me."

"That's enough," cut in Dad. "I don't want to hear another

word about zombies today, do you understand? Otherwise there'll be no more *Zombie Zac* for a month."

"But—"

"But nothing. I mean it, Kai. No television. No comics. No T-shirt."

No Zombie Zac? That was a million times worse than being grounded.

"Don't worry," said Luli, squeezing my hand. "He seemed like a nice zombie to me. I'm sure his friends are too. They're probably just excited to see Switchback, like me."

Really? Was *that* what the chanting was all about? Some kind of zany zombie welcome song? I'd just have to hope Luli was right.

Chapter 14

Saturday, April 30, 12:20 p.m.

The crowd in Polestone Park was growing increasingly restless. Mr. Patel checked his watch, humming the tune to "Pinball Wizard" under his breath, while Jermaine's mom scrolled through messages on her cell phone. The others stared up at the empty stage with equally worried expressions. But instead of the statue and concert they'd come to see, the only thing showing on the big screen was a coat rack.

"I knew it," murmured Kai, his eyes wide with worry. He looked around for the nearest police officer. "That chant I heard wasn't a zombie welcome song at all. They were just singing through today's menu." He let go of Luli's ankles, leaving her swaying precariously on his shoulders, and grabbed hold of Mr. Longdrone's elbow instead. "Switchback's in danger, sir. We have to warn him."

"Danger?" said the principal. "What kind of danger?"

Kai's friends pricked their ears, waiting to hear more.

"Zombies, sir," said Kai. "I saw them this morning—all twelve of them. *They're* the ones that took the statue, I'm sure of it. They must have taken it to practice with."

Luli clung onto her brother's hair as he demonstrated the zombie dance for everyone.

Mr. Longdrone looked bewildered. "Practice?" he repeated. "Zombies? I'm not sure I quite follow."

Kai tried again. "There's a scary gang of zombies in town, looking for some brain food. And I don't mean fish or avocados. It's Switchback they're after. They must have stolen the statue during the night to work on their attack strategy. And then Mr. Dearlove—he's one of the zombies—must have gotten carried away and taken a bite. *That's* what he was doing at the dentist's this morning. Getting his tooth fixed after he broke it on the statue's head."

"Zombies, eh? That's quite the imagination you've got there," said the principal, smiling to himself, while the others exchanged glances behind Kai's back.

"I *saw* them, sir." Kai was getting increasingly agitated. "And so did Luli. You saw the one in the dentist's, didn't you?" he asked, addressing Luli's left knee.

Luli tightened her grip on her brother's hair and nodded. "He certainly *looked* like a zombie. A nice one though. He didn't even *try* to eat us."

"That's because he was saving himself for lunch," said Kai. "We have to warn Switchback before it's too late."

Mr. Longdrone didn't seem convinced. "I don't think he's in any danger. If there really are zombies on the loose in Switchington Falls, I'll eat my hat."

"You're not wearing a hat, sir," Jermaine pointed out, grinning as if it was all a joke.

"Well, I'll eat my tie then, in that case."

"Not that it matters anyway," added Jermaine, his grin fading. "I don't think it was zombies who stole that statue. It was Mom's book group."

"Pardon?" said Mr. Longdrone, thinking he must have misheard.

"Huh?" said Kai.

"What?" cried Jermaine's mom, looking up from her cell phone. "That's crazy. Where on earth did you get that idea?"

"I heard you all last night, after I'd gone to bed," he told her. "While you were downstairs finishing up the last bits of chin."

"You were eating *chin*?" Kai stared at his friend's mom in disbelief, the trembling in his legs starting all over again. "Don't tell me you're a zombie too, Mrs. B? Oh help, this is worse than I thought."

"Don't be silly," said Jermaine. "Mom's not a zombie. They were eating cake—Switchback cake. No, Mom's not a zombie," he repeated. "Just a thief. You need to call Gloria and the others and get them to bring the statue back," he told her, his eyes filling with tears, "before it's too late. Please, Mom, I don't want you to go to jail. I don't want to live with Aunty Lena. She doesn't make me laugh like you do, and she's a terrible cook."

Jermaine's mom looked as confused as everyone else. "No one's sending me to jail, sweetheart. Why would you think that? Why would you think *we* had the statue?"

"I *heard* you," Jermaine insisted. "I heard you planning out the whole operation while I was lying there. Not the bit about the coat rack," he admitted. "I didn't know you were going to swap the statue for *that*, but it all makes sense now. Decluttering the hall was just a cover story, wasn't it? It must have been, because I went in the garage this morning, looking for my spare football, and the coat rack was gone. And now I know where."

"That's because Lena picked it up first thing this morning," his mom said, "while you were still in bed. They might look the same, but that's not our coat rack. Trust me. And as for what you heard last night—about how we were going to keep Switchback for ourselves—that was just us goofing around. You know what we're like when we all get together."

Jermaine shook his head. "No, not that part. I'm talking about later. I heard someone saying they had to get here before everyone else, so no one would notice . . . so no one would spot them taking the statue—that *must* have been what they meant. And then I heard you telling them to park nearby for a quick getaway. It was just like in my dream, only it was the statue you were planning to kidnap instead of Switchback." He broke off, looking confused. "Hey, why are you laughing? This is *serious*, Mom. You could get into so much trouble."

"Oh, Jermy," said his mom, wrapping her arms around him. "I'm laughing because it's the craziest thing I've ever heard. Me and the book club girls in some secret statue-stealing conspiracy? Don't be such a noodle! We were working out a way for Gloria and Marcie to see Switchback and still get back to Riddlingford in time for their concert. *That's* what you heard. The plan was for them to get here really early so they could get a prime parking space nearby, ready for a quick getaway. And then they were going to slip off halfway through while the roads were nice and clear. We said it wouldn't matter if they left before the end—no one would notice. They messaged me just now to say they've given up waiting and have left already. Such a shame."

"Really?" Jermaine looked relieved. "So you're not on any Most Wanted lists? You haven't committed any crimes? Apart from your dancing, I mean—that really *ought* to be a crime."

His mom shook her head, still laughing. "I don't know what happened to that statue, but it has nothing to do with me, I swear."

"It was the Meaner Lisa gang," piped up Mishka. "*They're* the ones who took it."

"The who?" chorused the others.

"No," said Mr. Patel. "It can't have been the Who, because they're not playing today. I already checked. And neither are the Police."

Mishka rolled her eyes. "This is *serious*, Dad. We're talking about dangerous art thieves—they've been stealing paintings and sculptures right across the country, and now they're here, in Switchington Falls."

"Ah yes, the Meaner Lisa gang," said Mr. Longdrone. "That's right. Miss Monnay was telling me about them in the staff room yesterday."

"Well, I *saw* them yesterday at the art gallery," said Mishka, shivering at the memory. "But no one believed me. I even *talked* to them. They wanted to know all about the security for the statue." *If only Mom and the receptionist had listened to me*, she thought. *If only they'd called the police then and there, they might have been able to save Picassa's artwork and the concert.*

"You didn't tell me that," said Catalina, clasping her friend's shaking hand in hers. "What did they look like?"

Mishka thought for a moment. "They were disguised as art geeks, with old-fashioned artist berets and sunglasses on to hide their features. But one was tall and bearded—there was no disguising that—with a scar on his left cheek, and the other one was short and round, with a large nose and dimpled chin."

"Like those two, you mean?" asked Jermaine, pointing up at the big screen.

Mishka looked up to see two men in dark suits and sunglasses approach the camera.

"Ladies and gentlemen," said the first man, stroking the scar on his cheek. "My name is Detective Henderson, and this is my colleague, Detective Rolfe, lead investigators on the recent spate of art thefts across the state. We'd like to thank you for your continued patience and cooperation today." The short, rounded man beside him nodded in acknowledgement. "We'd also like to assure you that we're doing everything we can to get today's event back on track. We'll be working closely with local officials to get to the bottom of your statue's disappearance as quickly as we can."

"So if anyone has any information . . ." added Detective Rolfe.

Down in the park, Mishka looked sheepish. "Yes," she admitted. "That's exactly what they looked like. I guess that explains all the questions they were asking. And the sketch they'd made of the art gallery. They must have been checking out the security in case the Meaner Lisa gang decided to target Switchington Falls."

"But you *were* right about the Meaner Lisa gang," said Jermaine, trying to make her feel better. "They must have been the ones who took it, if it wasn't hungry zombies or book club bandits."

"No. You're all wrong," said Catalina. "It was her," she added, pointing to the lady in the wide-brimmed hat. "It was Lisa La Loop."

The lady gave a start.

"*The* Lisa La Loop?" asked Jermaine.

"The one who played that balloon trick on Switchback?" asked Luli, peering down from her brother's shoulders.

"Shhh," said the lady in the hat, turning around to face them. She took off her scarf and sunglasses, and everyone gasped.

"It *is* you!" cried Mishka. "What are you doing here? What have you done with that statue?"

"You need to give it back," Catalina told her. "Otherwise the concert won't go ahead. I mean, I'd much rather it was *you* singing—I'm your biggest fan ever—but all my friends are here to see Switchback, and I don't want them to be disappointed. I thought you were planning something really cool," she added, with a disapproving shake of her head, "like parachuting out of a plane. But stealing's taking things too far."

"You don't understand," said Lisa La Loop.

"You're right," cut in Mr. Longdrone, treating her to one of his very best principal stares. The kind of disapproving stare that came free with detentions. "We don't understand. Why would you want to take our town's new statue?"

"Please," hissed Lisa La Loop. "Keep your voices down. I don't want people knowing I'm here, but not because I've stolen anything. I haven't even *seen* the statue. I'm just here to watch my boyfriend."

"Your *boyfriend*?" Mishka and Catalina looked at each other in surprise. "You mean . . . ?"

Lisa nodded. "Taz and I—I mean, Switchback and I—have been together for ages, but the record company wanted us to keep it secret, inventing this ridiculous rivalry between us instead. Apparently we sell more records as enemies than if people knew we were a couple. That's why they keep dreaming up publicity pranks for us to play on each other. They even wanted me to do something today, but I drew the line at that. Not in his old hometown. That wouldn't be fair." She looked up at the stage with a concerned expression.

"Poor Taz," Lisa continued. "He's been so looking forward to this—wanting it all to be perfect for his old friends and neighbors. He even had his new assistant come by last night to check everything was in place. I'm guessing the statue was still there then, otherwise Suki would have said something. Wait a minute, that looks like Suki up there on the screen now."

A bedraggled-looking lady with plaster dust in her hair loomed into view on the screen, her face pinched with worry. "I-I-I've got it," she panted. "It's over there by the stairs. The statue, I mean."

"My statue?" Switchback grinned. "Nice one, Suki!"

"My statue!" gasped Picassa. "Oh, thank goodness."

"The statue!" cried the crowds. "It's back! Hooray!"

"There's just one problem," said Suki, her lower lip trembling.

"A problem? What kind of problem?" Picassa pushed past Switchback and the mayor to get to the stairs, with the cameras following behind. "Noooooooooooo!" she howled, stamping her foot in horror. "What have you done to my masterpiece?"

"I'm so sorry," said Suki, as the camera zoomed in for a close-up of the statue's head and shoulders, and the angry black gash running all the way around its neck. "I was checking everything was in place last night and it toppled over and broke in two. I hardly touched it, I swear. I couldn't just leave it headless though—not with the big unveiling coming up—so I got some extra-strong glue and took it down to the basement to try and fix it. Except the janitor didn't know I was down there. He locked me in. I've been there all night, without any phone signal, screaming for help. He's only just opened the basement door now, and here

I am. I'm so sorry," she said again. "I didn't do a very good job mending it, did I? It looks even worse in the daylight."

"What about the coat rack?" asked one of the detectives. "How do you explain that?"

"I b-borrowed it from the coatroom to keep the velvet c-cover from getting creased," said Suki, her voice beginning to break. Fat tears rolled down her cheeks. "I'm s-so sorry, Switchback. I expect you'll be wanting a n-new assistant now."

Switchback's grin grew even wider. "No way. I love it! The crack around the neck reminds me of my biggest hit, "Losing My Head Over You.""

"Really?" asked Suki, sniffing.

"Really?" echoed Picassa, looking unconvinced.

"It's perfect," Switchback told her. "It's genius."

Picassa threw back her shoulders and patted her chest. "Yes. A crack around the neck was part of my original artistic vision, as it happens. I just wasn't sure Switchington Falls would be ready for that level of creative genius."

"So does that mean we can move on to the concert now?" asked Switchback, turning to Mayor Richards and the police officers.

"I don't see why not," said Detective Henderson.

"Bring it on," said Detective Rolfe, bopping for the cameras.

The crowds outside started cheering and whooping. (All except for Lisa La Loop, who was busy talking to someone on her phone.) They were still cheering—louder than ever—when

Switchback reached the outdoor stage, where he was joined by a troupe of familiar-looking zombies.

"It's Mr. Dearlove!" gasped Kai. For one horrible moment he thought the grizzly gang was going to attack the pop star live onstage in front of everyone.

But Switchback didn't seem remotely worried about his brains as he headed for the microphone at the front of the stage. "I'd like to kick this special performance off with a preview of my brand-new single, 'Zombie,'" he said, as his undead backup dancers got into formation behind him, starting up the chant Kai had heard at the old dance academy.

"Oh dear," said Mr. Longdrone, as Switchback launched into the chorus. "That's not very good."

"What's wrong with it?" asked Kai, his zombie worries forgotten. "I think it's kind of catchy."

"The song's brilliant," said Mr. Longdrone, wiggling his hips in time to the music. "It's having to eat my tie I'm worried about. Zombies loose in Switchington Falls . . . what's next?!"

Everyone laughed. (Everyone except Lisa, who was still talking on her phone, muttering about favors and making someone's day.) They laughed and sang and danced themselves silly, cheering like crazy when the song finally ended.

"And now," said Switchback, "I'd like to perform my all-time favorite, 'Losing My Head Over You.' This one goes out to a special someone watching in the crowd today." A stagehand appeared beside the pop star, whispering something in his ear. Switchback nodded. "And I'd also like to invite some special new friends to join me up here onstage for this one."

"That's you guys," hissed Lisa, putting down her phone and nudging Catalina with her elbow. "It's all arranged. Enjoy!"

Two more stagehands appeared in the crowd to lead the kids up onto the stage, with Jermaine's mom and Mr. Longdrone in hot pursuit.

"Oh my goodness, oh my goodness," said Mishka as Switchback welcomed them onto the stage. "This is the best day *ever*!"

"I know," agreed Catalina, waving to Lisa. "Thank you!"

"Woohoo!" called Catalina's dad from the back of the crowd, as her mom and great grandma waved in excitement. "Go Cat! Don't forget the bus move, honey!"

"The bus move?" asked Switchback. "I like the sound of that. What do you say, Switchington Falls? Are you ready for the bus move?"

"You bet we are," said Mr. Longdrone, removing his suit jacket and dropping into a low squat, hands already in the steering wheel position. "Hit it, Taz! Let's go!"

About the Author

Jennifer Moore is a British freelance writer and children's author. She studied English literature at Cambridge University, followed by a Research Masters at the University of Strathclyde in Scotland. Her fiction and poetry have been widely published on both sides of the Atlantic, and she was the first-ever UK writer to win the Commonwealth Short Story Prize. She lives in a small Devon town on the edge of Dartmoor and is an active member of the Society of Children's Book Writers and Illustrators.

About the Illustrator

Courtney Huddleston lives in Houston, Texas, with his wife, two daughters, and two cats named Lilo and Stitch. When he's not in his home studio working, he can usually be found playing video games, drooling over the work of other artists, going on long walks, or playing pranks on the family. While he gets inspiration from everything around him, his favorite way to get inspired is through travel. Courtney has been to most of the states in the United States, and he has visited more than a dozen other countries. He is currently searching for less expensive inspirations.

CAN YOU GUESS...
WHAT HAPPENED?